Finding Happiness

A Collection of Personal Essays

Natasha Borah Khan

ISBN 978-93-5610-544-7
© Natasha Borah Khan 2022
Published in India 2022 by Pencil

A brand of
One Point Six Technologies Pvt. Ltd.
123, Building J2, Shram Seva Premises,
Wadala Truck Terminal, Wadala (E)
Mumbai 400037, Maharashtra, INDIA
E connect@thepencilapp.com
W www.thepencilapp.com

DISCLAIMER: *The opinions expressed in this book are those of the authors and do not purport to reflect the views of the Publisher.*

Author biography

Natasha Borah Khan is an avid reader and has been penning down her thoughts as a blogger for more than a decade now. She has experimented across the writing spectrum with short stories, poetry, and articles, in addition to her signature personal essays and book reviews. Her work has also been featured in e-magazines and blogging forums.

Natasha is native to the beautiful state of Assam, where she has spent her formative years. After spending almost a decade in New Delhi where she started a life with her husband, she now calls Hyderabad her home.

After twelve years of corporate life, Natasha decided to press the pause button to raise her toddling daughter. She believes in the simple pleasures of life.

Apart from reading and writing, she also makes time for gardening and creative projects.

Website: https://natashabk.com/.

Facebook: natashaborahkhan

Instagram: @nats_bk

Twitter: @nats_bk

CONTENTS

Epigraph

For Ma and Deta...

Thank you for the gift of reading.

Acknowledgements

I would like to start by thanking all the people who have read everything that I have written over the years, especially my darling sister Namrata (who is also my greatest critic), my sweet Ma, my beloved husband Azhar, my dear friends, especially Priyanka, Lalita, Arunav and Madhusmita.

Azhar, this book would not have materialized without your firm and encouraging nudges over the years. You have finally succeeded in pushing the author you see in me out into the big bad world! Thank you, my little angel, Amaya, for being the most understanding two-year-old. The butterfly on the book cover is for you.

Daddy and Mummy, thank you for always looking out for me.

And finally, I would like to thank Team Pencil for bringing my words and thoughts to life.

1. Life Ain't Smooth, Ever

"Ups and downs in life are very important to keep us going because a straight line even in an ECG means we are not alive." ~ Ratan Tata

The ultimate wish everyone has, is to have a smooth life, isn't it? Half of my life has gone by (assuming an optimistic life expectancy!) and the one thing I have learned for sure is that life is anything but smooth. It is never the cakewalk we dream of.

They say, "When life gives you lemons, make lemonade". Some say, "grab tequila and salt", while the others say, "make orange juice and leave the world wondering how you did it". Easier said than done! Though, looking at the brighter side, it is hard but not impossible.

Life will always throw challenges at your face. It may be in the form of people, health, or even situations. You might have to stay or work with people whose wavelengths do not match with you... You might not be keeping well, or need to take care of someone who does not keep well all the time. You might be in a difficult relationship. You might have difficult children or relatives. You might have a difficult boss or subordinate. You might hate your job but need to continue due to financial burdens, and the list goes on… The challenges can be anything, but it is always up to you how you take them on.

We can crib, we can cry; or, we can simply take life head-on and turn each challenge into a life lesson. Instead of blaming God for all our problems and resigning to them as His will, we should remember that God helps those who help themselves.

Most of us are unhappy because we compare our lives with others, who we think are doing better than us. But everyone is fighting their own battles. All that glitters is not gold. So, you never really know, what they are going through beneath that shiny surface. And if at all you must compare, compare your lives with those who are lesser privileged than yourselves. Look for inspiration in people who are not as blessed as you (in terms of health, wealth or relationships) and yet make the best of their lives. Believe me, if you start counting your blessings, your problems will shrink away considerably.

I believe, problems and difficulties in any form are the ingredients that season our lives. We should not fear them but embrace them openly. Look for the positives even when you are in deep trouble. Find some humour in your situation. I like to do that. And at the end of it, we can only emerge from the situation stronger and more seasoned. Without problems, our life would just be bland, and we would never understand the true meaning of joy. And we humans never really appreciate things that come easy, do we?

2. The Fading of Handwriting

"Print is predictable and impersonal, conveying information in a mechanical transaction with the reader's eye. Handwriting, by contrast, resists the eye, reveals its meaning slowly, and is as intimate as skin." ~ Ruth Ozeki

Recently, I started noticing that my handwriting doesn't look the way it used to. Further, I realized that when I hold a pen my hand feels rigid and refuses to move across a page lucidly. I literally must force my hand to make my cursive right. My hand stiffens as I try to write… as if it were a freezing winter morning. The curves sometimes become sharper and at other times more slanted. It is also becoming increasingly difficult to put down my proper signature on official documents. This worries me.

When was the last time that you had written a long note by hand? All the writing that we do these days is small notes here and there. We do not even use a pen in days. All-day long, we find ourselves tapping away on the keyboards of our desktops or laptops and smartphones. Previously when I had to go shopping, I would scribble down a list and place it in my bag. Now I make that list on my phone. In fact, I make all kinds of lists on my phone... The practice of writing by hand is on the decline for sure. My imagination fears that one-day mankind would no longer know how to write by hand and typed words would become the new handwriting.

Writing has been a cornerstone of human civilization. From time immemorial, man has documented and shared experiences through journals, letters, and records. The discovery of manuscripts and documents from a bygone era still excites mankind. Will our typed and electronically written words excite our future generations about our age?

Typing away might be more convenient in today's world, but I believe writing by hand is more humane. Remember how in school, we were rebuked for our clumsy handwriting? Additional marks were given in tests for neat handwriting! I studied in a missionary school and was taught to write in cursive. Once, I saw a lady writing in specific cursive handwriting like mine and I couldn't resist asking if she did her schooling at a missionary school. And she indeed had!

And who can beat the charm of a handwritten letter! When my husband (then boyfriend) was away abroad for a couple of years, email and phone calls kept us connected. But still, I would write him a letter on special occasions. Handwritten letters are so much more romantic and intimate, aren't they? As a kid, my sister and I would write a lot of letters to our *Koka*, maternal uncles, cousins, and friends. We would then wait in anticipation of their replies. During the school summer and winter vacations, my then best friend and I would write to each other. And the vacations were just one month long. When one of my best friends in high school moved away to another town, we wrote to each other in codes, so that no one else would understand them.

While I was away from home in college, I used to write to my parents, sister, and friends. And the bank draft that I received from home would always be accompanied by a letter from *Ma*. Nothing can beat the sheer joy of opening and holding a handwritten letter. And what a joy to open a yellowed letter after many years! Treasures, aren't they? Today, in a world of instant messengers, that too at our fingertips, letters have lost their way.

With constant access to technology, conscious efforts are required to use a pen and paper. I try to write down to-do notes every day. When I feel like writing a post or an article, I do that virtually as it gives me the ease of editing and rewriting without leaving struck-out words or sentences. It becomes a fair copy without having to make one. Now that I have gone back to journal writing, it makes me write long notes from time to time. Most people today maintain e-journals (including video journals), once again eroding the age-old charm of handwritten pages.

In the present day, where kids are learning to use technology first and the alphabet later, writing by hand seriously seems to be the secondary writing practice. Increasingly, we are curbing ourselves of the three-dimensional freedom we have with pen and paper. The fading of handwriting is indeed a saddening and scary thought.

3. The Turning Point

"The turning point really is just knowing you're an imbecile."
~ Warren Cuccurullo

It was the end of my first semester of graduation, and I was home for a winter break. I was studying in Kolkata, which was the first metro city I stayed in. I am a small-town girl, so studying in a metro city was a new experience altogether. Suddenly, the world felt bigger and I, too, felt like a big girl. I couldn't wait to share my experiences back home.

At the first instance, I started to brag about my life in Kolkata to my *Aita* of all people! Among other things, I exclaimed to her, "You know *Aita*, I watched that blockbuster movie at the cinema hall and the cost of one ticket was one hundred and twenty rupees!" It was an expensive ticket and where I came from, a movie ticket used to cost around ten to fifty rupees only.

I thought *Aita* would respond in awe saying, What? Really!" But to my dismay, she responded sternly, "Aren't you ashamed of yourself? Your parents are making sacrifices here to educate you, and you are wasting their hard-earned money on movie tickets that expensive!"

During the time of my higher education, our family was going through a rough financial patch. My sister is just one and a half years younger than me which meant that our education expenses were double and simultaneous. But our parents never compromised on our education. While *Deta* had his steady job, *Ma* tried to make ends meet with creative endeavours and by becoming an active insurance agent later. They sent us girls to a private college in the nearest metro city. Our tuition fees and living expenses were not very high, but still, we couldn't afford it on our own. We took an education loan of a couple of lakhs of rupees which *Ma* and *Deta* repaid later. Also, *Koka* and *Aita* took care of us in ways more than one.

As a kid, my sister was always the sacrificing one. Even before we went away to college, she would hardly indulge herself. I, on the other hand, would not like to feel left out when my friends would make plans of eating out or watching a movie. I would indulge myself despite knowing that we couldn't afford it and I should not be wasting precious money. Today, when I look back at my younger self, I truly feel ashamed of my immature behaviour.

During my graduation, I was away from home for the first time. It was an exciting time of my life, tasting freedom away from the parental gaze. It was easy to get carried away by looking at fellow students, spending pocket money on fashion and outings. I did follow suit in the initial months. And then my fateful encounter with *Aita* happened. And thank God for that!

Aita is a straightforward lady. She is strong, in the will as well in spirit. She doesn't think twice before calling the spade a spade. She is not fond of unruly children. So, thanks to our polite demeanour, she adored us. She allowed us to tag along on her social visits and outings to the market. But she never indulged us unnecessarily and I feel that is the best thing she did to us or taught us.

So, when *Aita* rebuked me for wasting my parents' hard-earned money, it was a tight slap to my conscience. With just two simple and direct sentences, she reminded me of my humble roots and put my attitude on the right track. I realized that there was no pride in fulfilling my wishes and desires at the cost of my parents' sacrifices; that the real pride was in making them proud of me and in taking care of their needs. I started studying harder and tried to relieve them of monetary burdens in the smallest ways possible. Instead of fulfilling my desires then and there, I made a bucket list of things that I would like to do or possess. When I finally started earning, there was no looking back. It was time to take up responsibilities. The items on my bucket list started to get ticked off slowly. I am not ashamed to admit, that the list is still open.

At an age, when it was so easy to drift away, *Aita*'s wise words of admonishment changed my life forever. A true turning point in my life. She changed the way I looked at things. At that moment, she made me a better person and a better daughter.

4. First Impressions

"I don't know if you've ever noticed this, but first impressions are often entirely wrong." ~ Daniel Handler

First meetings can be deceiving. We cannot judge a person based on a single meeting unless we are psychic. Yet we mostly go by first impressions. But beware, because our quick judgments may impact our lives forever.

As a kid we were always told, "The first impression is the last impression". But as I grew older, I experienced the opposite in many cases, in my personal as well as professional lives. Classmates who I abhorred in the initial days of college, turned out to be true and lasting friends. Women who sounded like progressive liberal women over the first cup of coffee turned out to be regressive and hypocritical. Candidates who seemed smart and hardworking in the interviews turned out to be over-smart and sluggish. A manager who sounded like a cool visionary turned out to be myopic with a twisted mind. There are even instances where people seemed impressive till they opened their mouths!

It is only after a considerable number of interactions that we can understand the true nature of a person. Sometimes it takes days, sometimes months, and sometimes even years to understand people truly.

It is a well-established fact that we are easily deceived by looks. Good first impressions might work briefly in business relationships, where you don't have to spend much time together and the only motive is to get the work done. But when it comes to personal relationships, be it familial or friendship, deceiving first impressions may affect life-long relations. When people start showing their true colours, it might already be too late, and you might get stuck with them for the rest of your lives! At work, you might have to work with unpleasant colleagues who may make you take tough decisions. It may even be possible to distance yourself from such people who are outside the family. But when such people are close family members or within your social circle, your lives continue to remain uncomfortably entwined.

So, while it is natural to be deceived by first impressions, basically due to the "primacy effect", it is not wise to be influenced so easily. We should learn and practice to evaluate people over time, and from varying aspects. Don't be quick to judge people, either negatively or positively. Take your time; take it slow. And you will save yourself a lot of headaches and heartaches in the long run.

5. If You Must Compare

"Comparison is the thief of joy." ~ Theodore Roosevelt

The problem with most of us is that we always want to live someone else's life. We set our so-called "happiness standards" based on the visible lives of others. We are haunted by their apparent "happy and happening" lives. Based on their visible lives around us, especially on social media, we define our own lives. This is not right. We don't even know, how real their actual lives are… we are simply blinded by what they seem to have, and we don't! In the process, we choose to ignore and nullify what we already have. And thus, begins our unhappiness.

We are sent to school and college by our parents with great hope. We look at our peers and choose to compare ourselves to those we perceive to be leading better lives. We want to fit in; we desire to be them. We like what they wear, and our clothes start looking shabby. We desire to go out as often as they do. Instead of spending on our necessities, we start spending our pocket money on matching standards... We start forgetting the sacrifices of our parents. We start asking for more. But never once, it crosses our minds to compare ourselves with those peers who are less privileged than we are. Neither do we look beyond the superficial happiness of our "better" friends and try taking a peep at their real selves.

We start earning. But it's never enough. We choose to spend all of it on ourselves to match our upgraded 'happiness standards'. The bare necessities of life take a backseat. We desire to fit in among our new and better 'peers'. In our minds, we are still comparing our lives with our old and new friends. When our pockets are empty, we go to our parents! We don't even realize that now it's, in fact, our turn to take care of them! We continue to take them for granted.

We start our own family with our spouses. 'Happiness standards' are upgraded once again. We compare our standings with that of our siblings, relatives, friends, and colleagues. We even compare our spouses and children with that of others instead of focusing on the good in them. Instead of giving importance to our familial responsibilities or values and principles, we continue giving importance to maintaining our superficial images and status.

We continue to spend our money on branded clothes and accessories, throwing parties, gifting our well-to-do friends and relatives in a desire to receive expensive gifts and favours in return, looking down upon our less privileged relatives and friends. We even end up taking financial loans to maintain our lavish lifestyles and to take foreign vacations. We don't understand our spouses and children but click 'happy' photos to post on social media, hinting at love and happiness. We still don't care much about our parents. We still look at them as caregivers, free nannies, and free loan givers.

We are doing everything that our 'happy' peers are doing. But somehow, we are still not happy. We are striving and slogging to provide our spouses and children with all luxuries, but somehow, they are not happy with us and still complaining!

We do not understand that happiness is in our own hands, that we can never be happy if we set superficial and abnormally high, materialistic 'happiness standards'. We still do not understand that instead of running after money and success, if we started focusing on working hard and bettering ourselves every day, all kinds of successes are bound to follow. In our quest of looking towards the superficial upwards, we never choose to compare ourselves with the ones who are less privileged than us. But if we ever do so, we will be grateful for everything that we do have.

Think about those who must struggle each day for the basic needs of food, clothing and shelter. Think about those who can't even afford to go to school or college... Think about those who are the only earning members in the entire family and worse, they don't even have a job but have mouths to feed!

Think about those who are not blessed with health. They have a terminal or perennial illness, or deformities. Think about what they and their families have to go through… every single day. Think about those who don't have elders to fall back on, or worse, they have not even been blessed with a family.

If we need to compare at all, why don't we compare our lives with someone who is less blessed than us and count our blessings?

Why don't we start comparing ourselves with better spouses, children, parents, or friends and strive to be better persons ourselves? If we really must compare, let us compare with what really matters...

6. Winter Warmth

"Winter sunshine is a fairy wand touching everything with a strange magic. It is like the smile of a friend in time of sorrow."
~ Patience Strong

Sunshine during the day, oranges in the afternoon, and a cosy fireplace in the evenings. That is how I have always known winters to be. That is how we spend winters in Assam. That is how I wish my winters to be each year.

I grew up in the educational town of Jorhat, located in upper Assam. As young children, the annual book fair was the most awaited winter event for us. *Ma* used to get us mostly Assamese storybooks as she wanted us to have a good grasp over our mother tongue and not forgo it. Thankfully, her father, our doting *Koka*, would take us to the book fair too and get us any book we wanted, which were mostly English storybooks. During our school winter vacations, we used to eat our breakfast sitting in the winter sun on woven bamboo stools in the backyard. And then, it would be time to read our new books still sitting in the sun, dragging the stool to wherever the sun smiled.

When the new year was around the corner, the woven mat would be spread out on the front lawn. Art paper, pencils, eraser, colours, and other stationery would be brought out. It was time to make new year greeting cards. As the day progressed, and the trees cast changing shadows, the mat would be dragged and re-positioned.

Post lunch, the front lawn was shadowed, and the sun would shine on the front porch steps and veranda instead. We would sit there with oranges and the board of Chinese checkers. Blankets, quilts, and pillows were put out in the sun from time to time, and nothing was cosier than sitting on them! The sun was followed all day long.

In the late afternoon, dry firewood was accumulated near the fireplace, in preparation for cold evenings ahead. Come evening, the fire would be lit up. Each time when hands would turn cold after using the cold water, they would be warmed up in the fire. Potatoes would be put inside embers to roast for snacking. Neighbours would visit each other, sit around the fire and chat the evenings away. Hot beverages and fried fritters would be passed around. On cold winter days, when heavy fog or rain hid the sun, fireplaces would be lit up in the mornings itself.

On New Year's Eve and the community dinner during *Magh Bihu* (the harvest festival of Assam during mid-January), people would sit around a huge bonfire since evening, taking meals right there and chat late into the night, until the last piece of firewood burned.

This December, Delhi was said to be at the coldest in one hundred and twenty years. I have been a resident of Delhi for almost a decade now. The only open space in our flat on the first floor is the small balcony, the only spot where sunlight falls. But taller buildings have been built opposite to ours and the sunshine is almost gone. And there is no open space to light a fire either. So, we find solace in the room heater now. The sacrifice of natural light and sunshine is the cost you pay for living in a concrete jungle, at least for the regular working-class like us.

While growing up, I had never imagined that basic things like sunshine, clean air, greenery, music of rainfall, and open space will become a luxury someday. I had always taken them for granted. I think most of us had. And here we are, all grown up and doing well by societal standards, yet hungry for the simple pleasures of being alive.

7. Miserable By Choice

"There are seeds of self-destruction in all of us that will bear only unhappiness if allowed to grow." ~ Dorothea Brande

There are days when you want to feel miserable… when nothing can cheer you up. These are days when you are capable of finding unhappiness in everything around you.

Or is it just me?

I had a long and good night's sleep last night. I am fresh and wide awake. I am looking forward to a bright day. Maybe I won't get late today.

As I was dead tired last night, I did not pack our lunch boxes. So… I decide to cook Maggi noodles with some veggies for lunch. Then I find the oven gloves are not around and are lying on the dining table. Despite repeated requests, things are amiss in the kitchen. I am already losing my cool... I am also fixing breakfast simultaneously. I gulp down my breakfast and then pack the lunch boxes. My husband tells me to leave the utensils. He will do them. I am late. Again...

I rush to the bedroom to put on my jacket, shoes, and scarf. I am complaining aloud about things not being in order at home and how everybody is irresponsible. As I leave, my husband who is in the kitchen doesn't come to see me off, like he usually does. He hates it when I crib about home stuff. I climb down the stairs and realize I forgot my lunch. I go back.

So, I shall have to take an auto-rickshaw straight to the office again. At the stand, one driver quotes a charge which is far more than the metered charge. I get furious since I am already pissed off. He tries to bargain; I tell him in a little high-pitched tone that I am not going to pay him anything extra and walk away. The other auto drivers tell the guy that I am a regular and that he should not have quoted an unfair rate. I am called back. Once I settle down in the auto, I start to introspect on why the hell I took out a part of my foul mood on the poor driver. I rarely shout at auto-drivers, no matter how outrageous they are.

I reach the office in the nick of time. It is a hectic day at work. I am running up and down all day. It's sickening how senior people play cheap political games. My desk is strewn with papers and my mind is trying to do several things at once. It's amazingly frustrating how you are expected to build Rome in a day, that too single-handedly. And you are never good enough.

It's a long commute back home. I am dead tired. My dear husband has come to pick me up from the metro station. He is still in his office attire. He had reached home later than his usual time. Still, he came to get me from the metro railway station. But it's not cheering me up. I don't feel like talking. He suggests that I have an early night like last night. He drops me home and goes to see an unwell relative.

The main door is ajar. The house is in a mess as usual. I go straight to the bedroom. Automatically, I start focusing on all the negatives around me. There are so many positives. They outweigh all negatives. But no, I don't want to think about them today. My eyes brim up. I want to be miserable tonight. So just let me be...

8. Thinking Of My Favorite Teacher

"One looks back with appreciation to the brilliant teachers, but with gratitude to those who touched our human feelings. The curriculum is so much necessary raw material, but warmth is the vital element for the growing plant and for the soul of the child." ~ Carl Jung

The moment I think 'teacher', several faces start rolling in front of my eyes. I believe our first schoolteacher is the first outsider who tries to teach something to us as a child; the first person outside the family who influences us and affects our lives.

I don't remember the teachers from the first school I attended. I don't remember the first teacher I encountered when I went to Don Bosco, an institution where I spent a splendid eleven years. But I do remember most of the teachers after the kindergarten years. Some were kind, some were strict, some were indifferent, some involved, and some eccentric; some were even cynical. Of all our teachers, we love some and we hate some, right?

However, there is one teacher who immediately comes to my mind when I think of my beloved school. Dipti Ma'am. She taught us Science and Mathematics in high school. I believe she has been with the school since its inception years. To me, she is synonymous with my school life. She is my answer to the question, "Who is your favourite teacher?"

Dipti Ma'am was our class teacher when I was in the seventh standard. She is the kindest and most loving teacher I have ever known. You know how students get unruly and naughty in high school. But she was never harsh to any student. At least I had never seen her in that avatar. She was most patient and very soft-spoken. And of course, she was thorough with the subjects she taught.

Students are very cynical about their teachers. We used to criticize teachers' behaviour, personalities, and teaching styles at the drop of the hat. We would mimic their peculiar mannerisms and crack jokes (Well, I believe all teachers know this). But Dipti Ma'am was one teacher about whom all students spoke with reverence and respect. I have never heard any of the students speaking about her with any kind of disrespect. All we could mimic of her was her kindness and calmness.

Not to brag, but while in high school, I had become quite adept in mathematics. And twice I scored the full hundred marks when Dipti Ma'am was teaching. She applauded me in her way, by gifting me books on both occasions with personal inscriptions. Being a bookworm since childhood, nothing motivated me more. But above anything, I felt honoured. I still have the books in my maternal home.

While in seventh or the eighth standard, one of my friends had just learned pen calligraphy. She had special pens for the purpose. Once she brought her pens to school and the whole gang started giving her a notebook each so that she could inscribe our names on the same. Mine was the science notebook. The same day or a few days later, I don't exactly remember, we had to submit our science notebooks to Dipti Ma'am for corrections. When I got back my notebook, I was surprised to find my name inscribed in beautiful calligraphy, just below where my friend showed off her newly acquired talent. It was intricate handiwork with a simple ball-point pen. The calligraphy was in old English style. My first reaction was being surprised, wondering where it came from. Then I concluded that Madam made it. I never thanked her or asked her about the inscription. I still don't understand why I didn't. Then it became too late in my opinion to say anything. Neither did she mention it. So, it was left at that.

A couple of years after moving to New Delhi, I wished her on Teacher's Day with an SMS. She replied with a callback. Apart from me, she asked about my sister too. When I told her that I got married two years back, she asked about my husband. She advised that understanding is the main ingredient and wished us well. It is amazing that after so many years and thousands of students, she remembers her students by name. I came to know that she had retired two years back. But the school authorities wanted her back and engaged her as the coordinator of the junior school. I told her that every student loves her immensely and that she should be attached to the school for as long as possible; that without her the school would not be the same.

In our lives, most of us have had a teacher, whom we look up to and who made a lasting impression. For me, that teacher is Dipti Ma'am without a doubt. I pray the Almighty blesses her with health and happiness. I am sure she would continue to touch young hearts just like she touched mine. Thank you, Ma'am, for blessing me with your love and lessons.

9. Help Yourself

"All the advice in the world will never help you until you help yourself." ~ Fred Van Amburgh

When I was a little girl, I remember *Deta* bringing a poster with a quotation on it. It said, "God helps those who help themselves." And the quote has stuck with me ever since.

I have seen so many people praying to God, begging Him and pleading with Him in their prayers to help them, but not putting enough or any effort themselves to solve their problems. As a kid, I remember a young aunt who had flunked her board exams for several years in a row. Each year before her exams, she would visit all the temples in town with plates laden with fruits and flowers, requesting the deities to make her pass her exams. I wish she had put half the effort into her studies instead of wasting precious time visiting temples.

There are people all around me complaining about their weight, indigestion, or any other health issue, but would not cut down on their quantity intake or the intake of food which are harmful to them. I shall cite my own example. I have a bad back. I need to exercise daily for my back. But I neglect it. So would God help me to keep my back fit, if I don't take care of it myself?

When we see our near and dear ones in trouble, we tend to advise them. They might be having problems with their health, job, relationships, or finance. We are likely to suggest to them some dos and don'ts. But what if they don't want to listen to us. What if they tell us to mind our own business? What can we do? Nothing. For example, a diabetic person has to understand that sweets are not healthy, and he needs to abstain from them. His family and doctors can only advise and request him not to have sweets, or at least consume them in very small quantities and only once in a while. However, they cannot help if the person consumes sweets behind their backs and does not help his health.

"You can lead a horse to the water, but you cannot make it drink." I love this quote for it's so true. I see live examples of it every day around me. I often quote it at home and sometime soon I might even be asked to stop! I saw the horse's version of this quote where it says, "You can lead a human to knowledge, but you can't make it think." Quite apt, isn't it?

After I quit my job back home and moved to Delhi after getting married, I have been frantically searching for a job. When I was leaving my previous job, people around me kept telling me not to worry and that I would bag another job easily. But it was not easy at all. Nonetheless, I kept trying and didn't lose hope. I kept going for interviews. I trust God helped me to get a part-time job and I believed He placed the full-time job a little farther ahead. I just needed to take my steps towards it. I listened to my well-wishers' suggestions because I knew they were trying to help me. Even today, when I am working towards a goal, I know God is there guiding me through it, provided I am helping myself towards it as well.

We all want better grades, better jobs, better relationships, better health, and better lives. But are we putting in the necessary efforts to achieve that? Are we working towards it? God is not going to push us towards our goals. We have to walk towards it ourselves and only then He can guide us. Go ahead guys, help yourselves because it is you who really can.

10. Connected Stories

"We are all storytellers. We all live in a network of stories. There isn't a stronger connection between people than storytelling."
~ Jimmy Neil Smith

Do you ever think about how many people you know, meet or simply see every day?

There are people that we know on a personal level. We know about their lives, their stories, and their families. Such people are usually family, friends, and colleagues.

Then there are those, who are mere acquaintances. These are people whom we meet almost every day but don't really know, the "hi and bye" types. They can be the grocery store cashier, security guard, office receptionist, cab driver, regular fellow commuters, peers at large, etc.

Also, there are people whom we just see or hear about. Every day as we go about our lives, we see people whom we don't know anything about. People on the roads, people we see while commuting, shopping, in hospitals, restaurants, and everywhere else we go. Then there are the people who are friends, family, colleagues, and acquaintances talk about. Such third person people, whom we have never met, but whose stories we know to a certain extent.

All of us together form a human web, each of us linked to the other by the virtue of chain relationships and social circles. Each of us has a story of our own. Every single one of them is unique, yet similar in more ways than one. All of us have a different tale to tell. Each one of us is on a different timeline and each one of us with a different deadline. Each story is full of emotions, struggles, sacrifices, compromises, and triumphs. Each story is dotted with failure and despair. Each story is rich in inspiration and hope. And yet, each day we go about without knowing about the stories around us. We go about without a hint what each of our stories can teach us as well how they are all woven together in this colourful tapestry called life.

11. The True Us

"I have never been aware before how many faces there are. There are quantities of human beings, but there are many more faces, for each person has several." ~ Rainer Maria Rilke

A sister has been nicknamed "mother" by her friends because of her caring nature. But surprisingly she is hardly caring towards her immediate family. A grandmother used to go to lengths to help relatives and the underprivileged. But she often failed to see the pain of her own children. An uncle is very helpful to all relatives and friends. But at times can be ruthlessly rude to his own mother. An aunt who is utmost soft-spoken to everyone outside but is often bitter-tongued to her own family. Another uncle is a very jolly person and makes people laugh but can be extremely bad-tempered at home.

Which is a person's true nature? The personality which is displayed to outsiders or the one that is known at home? Why is it so easy for some to love outsiders rather than your own kin? Or is it much easier to be unkind in words and actions towards our own family? Or perhaps we simply take our family for granted...

Is it because at home, we don't need to pretend to be a perfect person all the time. There is nothing to hide.

People around us know all about our past and present. They know who we are or where we come from. Several of them know us inside out. So, it is easier to be our real selves. It is easier to vent out our darker emotions when we are with those people to whom we are close. Our anger, our frustration, and our grief. On the other hand, happiness is something that can be shared with anybody nonchalantly.

When we go out and make new friends and acquaintances, we always try to start with a clean slate. They know nothing of our past or our shortcomings. We do not share those parts of our lives with them that we are ashamed of, or those we feel will put us in the poor light. We always make a conscious effort to portray ourselves as wonderful people, all positive, all smiling. We want to be a person that everyone loves and likes to spend time with. Sometimes even our closest friend would not know all about us.

Every one of us likes to be praised, to be remembered with fondness or even adulation. In this quest, we may tend to look outside the home. Overlooking the emotional needs of our closest family, we may try reaching out to the extended one, to friends, and even acquaintances with our generosity. But is it okay to do this? And why do we do this? Do we feel that we are not appreciated enough at home, are rebuked or humiliated for simple shortcomings, that our opinions don't matter, or we are not valued at home?

Then, it also becomes important that we appreciate our family members, that we don't ridicule their mistakes but help them to correct themselves, consider their feelings while deciding things, make them feel loved with kind words and gestures. Our actions are all inter-connected.

Charity begins at home, they say. If we are at our best at home, we can be at our best outside rather than the other way round. But easier said than done. At work, I am a serious kind of a person. But at home, I laugh and joke hard. On a regular front, I am not very easygoing and a kind of introvert. I can be extremely patient at work, tolerating irritants and nonsensical colleagues. But with my closest family, more than often I end up losing my temper. Believe me, I am not one bit proud of this. And I regret my words or actions, the moment they are said or done. But maybe because they know that I am not perfect and that I have no ill intentions, they choose to forgive me. But I also know that I can bare my emotions to them unabashedly without being judged.

Sometime before getting married, I had a tiff with my sister. In the flow, I said something hurtful to her and she was on the verge of tears. I apologized. But the damage was already done. After she recovered from the hurt, which I had caused, she gave me very mature advice. She said, "I know you since we were babies. So, I know you well, that you don't really mean the hurtful words you say, that there is nothing negative in your heart. But the people in your marital family don't know you, they don't know who you really are or your heart. So please watch your words and your tone with them."

The question remains, which is the true us? I believe when we are in our own skins, we are truly us, with all our shortcomings. In this self, we can become better persons. And, when we can better our base selves, our extended selves can automatically turn for the better. Then, all of it will be our true self.

12. Journal Therapy

"Writing in a journal reminds you of your goals and your learning in life. It offers a place where you can hold a deliberate, thoughtful conversation with yourself." ~ Robin Sharma

My sister and I started writing personal journals when we were super young, most probably lesser than ten years old. I don't remember who pushed us towards it. It must have been either *Ma* or *Koka*. People would gift us the corporate diaries, which they had received for the new year, and we would hop away grinning like a Cheshire cat with them. Sometimes they were small and sometimes larger. Apart from journaling, such diaries were used for other purposes like noting down lyrics of songs, separate for English and Hindi songs.

In the beginning, we would write only on special days. Like when we were invited to a birthday party, we would note down who all were there, what was on the menu, and what games we played. Then on our birthdays, we noted down who came and with what gifts!

As we became older and sibling rivalry set in, we wrote almost regularly. What happened at school, what we did, our feelings about anything or anyone, crushes, and whatnot! We kept our journals secret, locked away from each other. Our parents didn't have prying eyes, so they were not a threat. But we were to each other's journals. As gawky teenagers, we didn't share our feelings. Even though we were at the same school and only a class apart, we didn't discuss our friends, problems or anything. But we were curious as hell!! So instead of sharing stories and feelings, we resorted to reading each other's diaries stealthily. Funnily, when we fought and quarrelled, we would often end up spilling the beans about it. And then hell would break loose. Keys got hidden in more secretive places, the journals got guarded more ferociously.

I maintained my journal throughout my teenage years and college. Then somehow, I stopped. Several years went by before I started again. I usually wrote when I was unhappy and needed to lighten my heart. But then I stopped, again.

Looking back now I realize that it was a healthy habit. Teenage years especially is a difficult phase of one's life. The simplest of matters seems super complicated and the smallest of concerns seemed like a matter of life and death. Opening up to parents or siblings is often considered out of question. And friends may not always understand. Bottling up emotions and feelings may end up affecting mental health negatively. In such a scenario, venting out one's feelings in a journal can be very, very therapeutic. This holds in any age or phase of life.

Presently, I am at my parents' place. The original plan was to stay here for a couple of months, allow my body to recuperate post-delivery in maternal care, and then be back home. But the ongoing pandemic has hit us all like a storm that is refusing to abate. So, we are still here, all together, fortunately. We are left with no option but to take each day as it comes. And honestly, we are in the best place that we can be right now.

But as human beings we are complicated, aren't we? Motherhood can be overwhelming. Inability to move around can feel like being shackled, even though I am not the outgoing type. Not being able to plan the days ahead can be frustrating. Plus, I have been trying to understand a certain aspect of my life and going through a lot of conflicting emotions lately. In the process, I have resorted back to my original therapist, my journal. Frankly, it is helping me gain insights into my feelings, reasons for my emotional turmoil and to find answers. Most importantly, it is helping me to unburden my heart and clear my head to a great extent.

Journaling is often associated with adolescents and young adults. But factually, anybody can benefit from this meditative practice. One of my maternal uncles still writes regularly. A well-expressed journal can provide fruitful insights into your life because it's not necessarily just about documenting your life. It is a relationship you can have with your own self. It can even be a spiritual experience.

Maintaining a journal can promote a sense of well-being and positive mental health. when you write down your feelings, reflections, dreams, goals, joys, sorrows, anger, and fears without any hesitation, it clears your mind and connects your thoughts. It can show you what you were, what you are, and what you can be. It is a kind of self-talk that can unwind, soothe or even motivate you. It can also help you to understand yourself better and guide you to where you want to be in your life.

So, if you are someone who has a lot going on in your mind or heart but not being able to open up to anyone, I urge you to start writing a journal. It is very important to share what you are going through, no matter how silly or grave it may seem. And if you can't trust anyone at the moment, just let it flow in your journal. Trust me, you will feel a lot better.

13. One Day – Many Stories

"Every day brings new choices." ~ *Martha Beck*

One day – duration of a single rotation of the Earth. But it's a single day of the life of every single living being on this planet. And for a mayfly, it is its entire life.

On any given human day…

Someone is born. Someone dies.

Someone was waiting for it. Someone was dreading it.

Someone is happy. Someone is sad.

Someone is laughing. Someone is crying.

Someone is sound asleep. Someone is wide awake.

Someone is waiting. Someone just arrived.

Someone falls in love. Someone breaks up.

Someone is getting married. Someone is getting divorced.

Someone is tense. Someone is relieved.

Someone is enjoying it. Someone is suffering.

Someone is wasting food. Someone is hungry.

Someone is thankful. Someone is complaining.

Someone is mean. Someone is kind.

Someone is praying for the sun. Someone is praying for rain.

Someone gets promoted. Someone gets fired.

Someone passes. Someone fails.

Someone wins. Someone loses.

Someone makes peace. Someone fights.

Someone is living a fairy tale. Someone is living a war.

Someone loves. Someone hates.

Someone forgives. Someone avenges.

Someone is running from family. Someone is longing for one.

Someone is lonely. Someone wants to be alone.

Someone is charmed. Someone is disgusted.

Someone wins a lottery. Someone loses every penny.

Someone sees a ray of hope. Someone loses all hope.

Someone starts believing in God. Someone turns an atheist.

Someone is praying for another day of life. Someone can bear no more.

And when it ends, it had been one day and a million stories.

14. Struggles of Life

"Let perseverance be your engine and hope, your fuel."
~ H. Jackson Brown, Jr.

Someone I know closely and who is like a sister to me once said, "A girl either struggles before her marriage or after her marriage. I think I am struggling now." She was unmarried then. She was upset at home those days as she didn't get along with her brother's wife and her brother often gave her an earful at his wife's behest. But she lived with other family members who did love and care for her. As I listened to her, many faces crossed my mind, several being her own friends and family who were struggling to go on every day. I wanted to remind her of those. But I didn't. Most people don't like patronizing responses and they take it as a rebuke or even insult. So, I didn't say anything and simply smiled.

I meet and interact with all kinds of people in my personal and professional life. During recruitment processes, I have interviewed many candidates and worked with colleagues who had educated themselves through correspondence or part-time courses because their parents couldn't afford to educate them or they had to take on the responsibilities of their families at a young age. Some are the sole earning members of their families and are always short of money, let alone save a penny. I know bright people who couldn't pursue higher studies or complete their education at all due to financial constraints and familial duties. I know of siblings who skip school in turns so that they can take care of their bed-ridden mother. I know families where kids are always falling sick due to malnutrition. I know fathers who stay thousands of miles away from their families to earn so that their children may have better futures. I know families who are dependent on the generosity of relatives and friends to survive. Knowing such stories makes me grateful for what I have.

Then there are others who grew up or live in disturbed homes with abusive or alcoholic parents or spouses, orphans who are forced to fend for themselves from a tender age. Girls who haven't been allowed to study or follow their aspirations because of their gender, young women attacked, molested, or even killed because they dared to move forward. Their struggle stories make one tremble with emotion.

While commuting across the city I encounter so many autorickshaw drivers and cab drivers. Some drive two days straight while some work only at night as they make more money that way. They tell me that they remind their children to study hard and become capable of leading better lives than themselves. Some brim with pride as they share how intelligent their daughters and sons are. Most of them have migrated to the capital from other regions of the country. All of them work hard so that their families can have good lives and their children can have better futures.

Every day we come across motivational stories of children of economically backward families rising against all adversities and cracking civil services, becoming pilots, professors, doctors, engineers, scientists, athletes, and other successful professionals. Many of these children didn't have the luxury of even the basic amenities like a proper roof over their heads, electricity, two square meals, decent pair of clothes, new books, or even notebooks. We also hear inspirational stories of survivors of abuse, attacks, and ill-health who fought back and achieved heights while giving hope to others. Such stories remind me that I have been among the privileged and blessed.

The current economic situation due to the COVID19 pandemic has brought all kinds of struggles to the forefront. People are losing jobs and going out of business. With households to run and EMIs to pay, imagine the plight of the unemployed bread earners and their families. Migrant workers, rendered jobless, walking hundreds of kilometres to their native place with young children in tow are redefining the word 'struggle' itself. With educational institutions closed, classes are happening online for which one needs to have smartphones or laptops with access to the internet. Underprivileged students are killing themselves because they don't have access to technology and are being left behind by the system itself. On the other hand, there are students who go to private educational institutions, with their pocket money allowing them to shop and to go out with their friends frequently. They consider the latest wardrobe, outings, smartphones, laptops, and internet as basic needs; will they ever understand such lacks. What does struggle mean to someone who has always led a protected life, someone who hasn't known hunger, poverty, deprivation, discrimination, fear, or illness? What does it mean to someone who sleeps in an air-conditioned room in summer and has running hot water in winter?

That unmarried girl is married today. And I hope she never has to experience struggles worthy of being called struggles. But I do hope that she will be emphatic and considerate towards those with struggles far greater than hers and be humbled.

Yes, we all go through different kinds of struggles in our lives irrespective of our social standing. Our stories may differ, but inherently they all are the same. We continuously struggle towards living in ideal conditions, be it financially, socially, personally, professionally, physically, or mentally. So, should I be judging anybody based on what struggle means to them? Some struggles seem minuscule on our rating scale while others are extraordinary. Degrees vary, but for those experiencing them, all are struggles of life, nonetheless, aren't they?

15. Karma

"How people treat you is their karma; how you react is yours".
~ Wayne Dyer

'As you sow, so shall you reap' goes the old English saying. This is the very basis of 'karma', which simply states that if you give good, you will get good, and if you give bad, you will get bad. Although the philosophy of karma is known to be of Indian origin, karma is a universal phenomenon. What goes around, is bound to come around. All major religions of the world speak of karma in some context or the other.

According to the Vedas, if one sows goodness, one will reap goodness; if one sows evil, one will reap evil. Karma refers to the totality of our actions and their concomitant reactions in this and previous lives, all of which determine our future. Human beings act of their own free will, thereby creating their destiny. Hence, karma is not fate. A good summary of the theistic view (of the Vedanta) of karma is expressed by the following: 'God does not make one suffer for no reason nor does He make one happy for no reason. God is very fair and gives you exactly what you deserve'.

Gurbani's law of karma holds everyone responsible for what the person is or is going to be. We harvest exactly what we sow; no less, no more. Based on the total sum of past karma, some feel close to the Pure Being in this life and others feel separated. According to Sri Guru Granth Sahib, 'According to the karma of past actions, one's destiny unfolds, even though everyone wants to be so lucky'.

According to Buddhist Philosophy, karma is categorized within the group or groups of cause in the chain of cause and effect. Any action is understood as creating 'seeds' in the mind that will sprout into the appropriate result when met with the right conditions. Most types of karmas, with good or bad results, will keep one within the wheel of samsāra (cycle of birth), while others will liberate one to nirvāna (free from suffering).

Although Islam views all human dramas as the will of God, the Quran states that the good or bad fortunes that befall man are the results of God's reactions to man's actions.

Modern theorists argue that karma is very much predictable like other natural phenomena such as gravity and is devoid of any spiritual linkages. Sakyong Mipham eloquently summed this up when he said, 'Like gravity, karma is so basic we often don't even notice it'.

On the other hand, karma is also considered a myth and illogical. As the Burmese proverb says, 'Worthless people blame their karma'.

I believe in karma. And I see it in my everyday life very clearly. When something awful happens to me, I remember the times when I have been awful, in my behaviour, actions, and even thoughts. Whenever I am angry and hurt people with my words and behaviour, I often instantly accidentally hurt myself physically or forget my keys or cellphone while leaving home for work. Now that's instant karma, isn't it? The logical explanation will of course be that I was distracted.

I have seen that unkind and uncaring people often suffer from persistent physical ailments. When I am unkind to some relative, some other relatives are also unkind to me or treat me unfairly. I know people who had broken quite some hearts in their time and now are in marriages that lack love, respect, or support. I feel karma is all about positive and negative energy. Positivity begets positivity and negativity begets negativity.

From our very childhood, we are taught to be kind and good. We are taught not to do anything bad to not displease the Almighty and bring on His wrath. We are taught to be kind, loving, peaceful, and helpful because that would please God. These very simple teachings translate into the concept of karma, what goes around, comes back around, doesn't it? Whatever it is, spiritual, cultural, natural, philosophical, or illogical, karma is surely something to be pondered upon.

16. All Is Well

"Say you are well, or all is well with you, and God shall hear your words and make them true." ~ Ella Wheeler Wilcox

The day did not start very well. The baby fussed all night long. Waking up multiple times to nurse and soothe her had given me a headache by dawn.

And the heat. My God! The humidity. I have not passed a summer in so much heat and humidity in almost a decade. Such snobbery, you say! Am I not in my native place? Yes, I am. But I have not spent one summer here in so many years. Can't bear the weather of my own place? I am bearing it alright. Yes, I grew up in this region. But Jorhat is where I grew up and it is in the upper part of Assam. The climate is way better there than in Nagaon, where I presently am. Also, Nagaon is infamous for its humid weather. And, in case we have forgotten, climate everywhere was far better two decades back than it is today...

Long hours of power cuts and low power voltage is making the summer worse here. Continuous sweating and consequent prickly heat and body acne, followed up by itching and scratching have made our skin resemble that of the prized one-horned rhinoceros of our region.

The baby has been fed, cleaned, bathed, cleaned, fed, and cleaned. I managed to take my bath just before lunch. I was looking forward to taking a nap alongside the little one in the late afternoon, but she decided not to nap in this unpleasant weather. I tried to reason with her; actually, that is how the whole afternoon was eventually spent in case you are curious... But she did not relent. She spent her time crawling all over the bed, sometimes playing with her favourite board book and sometimes trying to scratch the peeling on the wall. She eventually came up to me scratching her head, ears, and eyes, making me hopeful that she was finally ready for her nap. She nursed but does not fall asleep. I scooped her up in my arms and paced the room, rocking her while humming her favoured lullaby. Several minutes passed and I put back her on the bed. Humming the lullaby had made me sleepy, but not my daughter. The last time I had slept for eight hours straight at night was in the hospital the day she was born!

They say, having a child changes your life. I thought it to be overrated. But no, my friend, it isn't. Parenthood changes your lives, and motherhood turns it upside down. Some days are good, some not so good. Today is not so good. Nothing feels right and I am feeling irritable. I am thinking about what has become of my life. I no longer have any control over my routine and activities. Today is making me teary-eyed. Even her one-tooth angelic smile is not melting my heart and mind a hundred per cent. No good.

It is evening now. The little one has been cleaned and fed again, like the many times during the day. She is overtired now but willing to sleep. The weather has cooled down a bit. But she will need help to fall asleep. After nursing, rocking, and pacing, she finally falls asleep. The ceiling and the stand fans together are keeping her cool. Meanwhile, her father has wrapped up his work for the day. He offers to stay with her and asks me to take a break.

I am outside. The air is much cooler now. Humidity has subsided to a large extent. But there is no breeze. I look up at the sky. It is clear, the countless stars twinkling and looking down upon me. I feel overwhelmed and my eyes well up. I do not understand why but it feels good. I feel blessed to witness such a beautiful sight. It takes me back to my early years when such a clear, starry sky was a regular feature of my life. I was so deprived of this pleasure and beauty all these years in Delhi, where the sky is always hazy.

Gazing up at the universe, the milky way, and the constellations make me feel minuscular. And the negative feelings that held me all day long, insignificant and futile. What are we in this infinite universe? Smaller even than a speck of dust. Our egos and problems are even smaller than that. Am I not blessed to be alive, healthy, and able to see the wonders of the world? Am I not fortunate to spend this difficult time of the pandemic with my loved ones and so close to nature? And my little one, who has brought so much joy and a new meaning to my life. Yes, I am blessed. All is well. And I mutter a silent prayer, thanking the Lord.

17. Music in My Life

"Music is the shorthand of emotion." ~ Leo Tolstoy

Most people around me do not know that I had trained in Indian classical music as a child. It was *Aita* who pushed my sister and me towards classical music. She is a good singer and knows how to play the harmonium. She is actually brilliant in all kinds of cultural activities, be it singing, dancing or drama. *Ma* and her two brothers also have beautiful voices and learned to play musical instruments as children.

Both of us sisters attended the music classes on weekends and practised regularly, but we were never very dedicated to it. Well, it lasted for five years and we did not continue it further. The reason for discontinuity was very silly, although it was not silly for my ten-year-old self and eight-year-old sister. To get a degree in music, you need to sit for exams like any other course. The practical part was fine, but the theory part was too cumbersome for us. Hours of writing notes in our mother tongue and then memorizing it was a bit too much. And the lack of passion to master it also played a part. I am not proud of my younger self though, for giving up.

But giving up on learning Indian classical music doesn't mean that we don't love music. I think music rules our genes! You can catch my mother humming some tune or the other all the time. My father still listens to music every evening. I used to solve math problems while listening to music. My sister and I shared a room, and we would take music breaks between our studies. We would switch off the lights, lay on our beds, and enjoy a song or two. We would save money to buy music cassettes and exchange with our friends and make copies. It was the era of pop music, Hindi, and English, and what a wonderful time of life it was.

I would listen to the latest Bollywood and pop music numbers before leaving for school because it was considered cool to know the lyrics when we sang them with our friends in school. I had two notebooks, one for writing down the lyrics of Hindi songs and the other for English songs. My sister and I would spend hours playing, pausing, rewinding, playing, pausing the music player to note down the lyrics and make sure that we got them right. Over the years, we developed tastes for music of different genres. But we still have our common favourites.

I have music for every mood. Sometimes I wake up with a particular song on my lips. And for the whole day, it will run on my lips in a loop. When I commute or move around with earphones, the whole world seems like moving scenes from a movie. My movements are in rhythm, and everything becomes beautiful. I love to do my household chores while listening to music. It adds a spring to my step. On days when I feel under the weather, my favourite songs pull me up. Music makes me happy and bad situations tolerable.

My husband too is a music lover and hopes to learn to play the guitar someday. He even has the guitar ready! We have our personal playlists, with many common songs, and they are a must when we take road trips. We like to enjoy music together and now we do that with our daughter. Hopefully, she too will grow up to share our love for good music and maybe share our tastes too.

18. Ulcers

"I have chosen to be happy because it's good for my health."
~ Voltaire

I have been diagnosed with two small gastric ulcers, one in my stomach and the other in my oesophagus. My doctor said that it is a common ailment in new mothers and is usually stress-induced. Along with the medicines, she advised me not to take the stress and stay happy.

Funnily, even before the endoscopy confirmed her doubts about the ulcers, the first thought that struck me out of nowhere was that my negative energy, which I have been harbouring over the past year has manifested itself and caused it. And when she mentioned stress, I knew for sure that I have brought it upon myself.

Thanks to the pandemic, I have been staying at my maternal home with my baby and husband for more than a year now. My husband is super involved in parenting, and I have all the support that a daughter gets at her mother's home. And yet, here I am, angry and frustrated for a good amount of time. Most people who know me will wonder why and might even secretly say that I am crazy. And maybe I am.

I left home for higher education when I was nineteen years of age. Since then, I have visited home in semester breaks while in college, and then intermittently for a few days since I started working. After I got married and moved away to another city, I saw my folks once a year for a few days. And sometimes, they visited me. Eighteen years since I have left the nest and flown away.

And then the year 2020 happened. My plan of spending my maternity leave in my native place has extended indefinitely primarily because we don't want to expose our little girl to the pandemic in a high-risk environment.

Frankly, after all these years, I have forgotten how to live with my folks. We have changed and remained unchanged in our ways, and undue friction happens from time to time. Short visits annually are always goody-goody and are spent in feasting and catching up. I have forgotten how to live with their eccentricities, especially that of my father's. We don't seem to agree on anything anymore! Our ideological differences are cracked open huge. His shortcomings which I laughed off as a teenage daughter, now put me at wit's end as a grown woman. My head just heats up and won't calm down until I let it out. Believe me, I am ashamed of my behaviour every time. But I just can't help it! It seems as if he can bring out the worst in me. *Deta* says that I have changed. I know he hasn't. So, it is probably me.

I would also spend my time and energy being angry with random relatives for their actions or inactions that don't conform to my idea of the right behaviour. I would imagine having fake arguments with them while in the washroom and have the last word in all of them. I have been angry with people for being who they are, and not somebody I would like them to be! Doesn't that sound ridiculous and sad? The whole time, I couldn't see my own behaviour, how I was becoming a bitter person, always angry and upset. The height of my rude demeanour slapped me hard when I found out that my mother was taking anti-depressants because she was so hurt by one of my passing comments. My sweet mother, who does everything to ease me out and support me in every little way possible, didn't even show me that she was upset with my irrational behaviour. And me, the monster of a daughter! I was so, so ashamed.

I usually consider myself to be a nice person and preach that we should be kind to everyone and that kindness is always possible. But lately, I have been so horrible to all the people who care about me the most in the world, my husband, my mother, my sisters. And my poor father. He is seventy years old now! What's even the use of being angry at him after all these years? What is the purpose of my unkind behaviour? What does that make me? A pretend?

Then I started retrospecting my behaviour, where it was coming from. Was it post-partum? Maybe, it is. Motherhood changes one's life. But I was prepared. Or was I? Taking a career break was my decision. Maybe, I had underestimated to what extent my life would change. A little life, my flesh, and blood, now dictates my life, even the time when I can answer nature's calls. I haven't slept even four hours straight for over a year now. I can hardly squeeze out time and opportunities to read, write or do something I would like to. It has been a year since I am at my parents' place, but I have walked around the garden only four to five times. In all this time, I have neither got the opportunity to sit in the winter sun and enjoy a book, nor had the opportunity to enjoy a hot cuppa looking at the rain. There are days when I miss going to work, getting things done, delivering solutions. I miss my payday. I miss wearing my regular clothes… I'm tired of wearing nursing ones. I miss binge-watching movies and shows with my husband, miss being in control of my routine. Does that make me a bad mother?

Honestly, my husband keeps me sane. Over the past year, he has counselled me innumerable times, pushing me to reflect on my behaviour, see the brighter side, count my blessings, to be kinder in my words and behaviour. He keeps telling me that there is always a better way to say and do things. Funnily, he is more chilled out here at his in-laws' than I am!

So yes, I have brought the gastric ulcers upon myself. And I know I alone have the power to heal them. Each day now, I am trying to heal my inner self. I am trying harder to focus on my prayers. I am trying harder to be kinder to people around me. I am trying to be more conscious about how I am speaking, focusing on my tone and the delivery of my words. In a situation where I am likely to flare up, I am trying not to engage and move away. And when I look at my little girl, I try to see all the ways that God has been kind to me and thank Him. I believe, my ulcers (the physiological as well as psychological) will heal and go away for good.

19. Lives Strive Together

"You are here so I can teach you something. All the people you meet here have one thing to teach you...That there are no random acts. That we are all connected. That you can no more separate a breeze from the wind." ~ Mitch Albom

April 2021. Every day, my country, India, is touching new heights in the number of Covid19 cases. Every day, more and more people are dying. Every day, we are hearing that someone we know has been infected. After one year, we are back to square one, that too a grimmer one. How did we reach here? When the rest of the world has contained the spread and is on a healing path, how did we manage to relapse and facilitate a stronger and harder second wave?

I have always felt that human life (forget about other forms of life) in my country has little value. And the poor handling and mismanagement of this pandemic have only fortified my view. Even at this critical hour, regional and central governments are busy playing politics. Aggressive vaccination drives haven't started yet. Even under-reporting of cases is not helping anymore. We had underestimated the deadly virus. Instead of bracing the nation and preparing for the worst, we are conducting elections. In recent months, we have seen massive campaign rallies, led by top leaders themselves, where all precautions against the pandemic had gone for a toss. We have been so ill-prepared and ill-equipped to handle the pandemic. Lack of hospital beds, shortage of oxygen, and medicines are echoing our inefficiency and incompetence, clear and loud.

And what about us, the common man? For the last few months, we have been reckless. We have hosted and attended weddings, parties, and other family functions and encouraged large gatherings. We have neither worn masks while going out, nor washed or sanitized our hands enough. We had perhaps even participated in political and religious rallies. While the frontline health workers have been risking their lives all this time, we have been audacious enough to negate their efforts in every possible way. Well, we don't fear the Covid19 infection and possible death but monetary fines do scare us. So now that fines are being imposed, we have finally started wearing the mask while going out. And now that we are seeing the overcrowded hospitals, shortage of oxygen and medicines, and the queues at crematoriums and graveyards, we are rushing to medical centres to get vaccinated.

And, as I mentioned earlier, for more than a year now, we have been staying with my parents in Assam, primarily to protect our baby girl more than anything else. We are staying put here in an attempt to elude the virus. But immediate family members and close friends are back home in Delhi as well as in other parts of the country, and they have been on our minds constantly these days. Some of them have also been infected. Right now, all we can do is stay careful and pray for everyone's wellbeing.

April has been a stormy month in Assam so far. In the aftermath of thunderstorms and hailstorms, I see leaves (old and young), flowers, and nascent fruits strewn all over the ground. Like these storms, the pandemic is hitting us hard and strong, equalizing us in death and suffering. A teeny-weeny virus has rocked the world and shaken us to the core. It is reminding us again and again how uncertain life is. I believe it is also God's way of telling us who the boss is. We have used and abused the Earth and its resources in a limitless manner. We have messed with Mother Nature's equilibrium and overstepped our boundaries.

At the micro-level, we spend so much time running after material milestones and waste so much time hating and disliking each other. We keep forgetting that life itself is above all personal differences and materialistic aspirations, that how we choose to live our life is the most important thing. I wish and pray that in this difficult time, we all can retrospect and reflect on our own lives and actions. I hope we forgo our ego and take the first step to make amends.

In the current situation, we can't do much about the lack of hospital beds, oxygen, and medicine. What we can do is try to stay home and stay safe. Please remember that being able to stay at home today is a privilege. Most of us have to go out and risk infection to earn our livelihoods. We can check on our family and friends regularly, forget our differences, be kind and empathetic, help each other however and whenever possible, and come together as a family and community.

As the smartest species on this planet, we can pledge to reduce, reuse and recycle. We should try, learn and understand that all lives, irrespective of forms and species, are important for our survival. None of us will strive without the well-being of the other. Our entire universe has been created with delicate balance and it is our responsibility to keep it that way. Else, Mother Nature will take matters into her own hands, time and again, to set things right.

All lives in this world are connected. As an individual, our well-being is connected to the well-being of our family and friends. As a community, our well-being is dependent on the health of our society and nation. As a species, our survival is dependent on the survival and existence of all other species and life forms. It is only together that we can strive. With imbalance and selfish motives, we only risk our very existence.

P.S.- It is January 2022 now. We are learning to strive along with the virus, changing the very ways of how we are going about our day-to-day lives. The world is now reeling under the third wave of the pandemic, facing the threats of new strains every day. The virus is adapting to immunizations and mutating rapidly. But we are still largely reckless, still putting ourselves and others at risk. Even though we are still praying that the world goes back to normal, we are not playing our part very sincerely.

20. Book-Smitten

"Books are the quietest and most constant of friends; they are the most accessible and wisest of counselors, and the most patient of teachers." ~ Charles W. Eliot

I have been in love with books for as long as I can remember. As a kid, when I used to visit my relatives and family friends, I would ask for a book (in relevance to my age of course) and settle with it in a corner and be engrossed in it for the whole time.

I guess I have got my love for reading from my parents. Both are avid readers and we have always been surrounded by books. While growing up, I saw that the last thing *Deta* did before going off to sleep is read. And I, too, have inherited this habit. *Ma* always finds some time to read something or the other during the day, no matter how busy she is. My sister and I used to compete (and we still do), as to who can read which book first and threaten the other to disclose the ending.

With books as my companions, I have travelled far and wide. I have been enchanted by fairies and pixies, lived the life of a boarding school, solved mysteries and discovered new places, laughed and cried with the characters, walked along the corridors of history, charmed by the princes and princesses, mesmerized by the striking similarities of different faiths, exalted and disparaged famous and ordinary lives alike, but have drawn lessons and knowledge from all.

There is a book for my every mood. Reading makes me forget all the worries of life and transports me to a different world altogether. As a child, I was a huge fan of Enid Blyton's books. I think I have read all her books available in our school library. As a kid, her stories of fairies and magic were a treat. How I wished that I too had a little fairy or a pixie for a friend. As I grew older, her boarding school tales and mystery-solving children replaced the fairies. We also read 'Tinkle', 'Panchatantra' tales, and '*Burhi Aair Sadhu* (Old Grandma's Stories)'. Then came the season of Nancy Drew and Archies, followed by Mills & Boons and Sidney Sheldon. As a young adult, I started reading biographies, religion, philosophy, and semi-biographical novels. Today, I love to read memoirs, historical and mythological fiction, well-researched fiction, nonfiction, and personal essays.

When my sister and myself were quite young, *Koka* and *Aita* gave us a trunk that was full of storybooks belonging to *Ma* and her brothers. At home, my father has a small library. So having known the joy of books, I promised myself that I would get myself at least one book a month when I start earning. And today I can boast of a decent collection, myriad of books across genres. I am glad to share that my love of reading has rubbed off on my husband too and now he enjoys books, but strictly the nonfiction genre.

My wish for my daughter is that she will also be an avid reader. When she was born, a book was my first gift to her. Since then, we have got her age-appropriate books, and she does enjoy them. I carve out a reading time each day when she and I both can spend time with books. She loves to flip through the hardbound fat Britannica and pulls my or her father's index finger to point at different pictures in it demanding that we tell her which is what. She is almost two and learning new words every day.

I believe I have been smitten by books for life. With them, I am never lonely. Reading makes me happy and a student for life. And being lulled to sleep by a book at night is my perfect ending to an imperfect day.

21. Finding Happiness

"Happiness depends upon ourselves." ~ Aristotle

While in school, we had to read a poem by Ananda Chandra Agarwala as a part of our Assamese language curriculum. The poem was titled *"Sukh"* meaning "Happiness". It was a long poem where the poet talks about how a man pursues happiness and encounters only unhappiness in the process. He writes how man fails to see that his happiness is in his own hands and that happiness runs after a person who can sacrifice his selfishness. He further writes that if one can be kind and charitable to others in the world, there will be no unhappiness in the world. It has been more than two decades since I had to study that poem, but the first few lines of the poem are still etched in my memory. And maybe after all these years when now I am approaching my middle age, I can finally see sense in the poet's words.

Most of us feel that we can be happy if we can have something which we don't have presently. It may be a house, a car, designer clothes, gadgets, appliances, vacations, in short, more money to fulfil our material desires. We might have set certain expectations from our partners, family, friends, and job, but they are not living up to it. Hence, we are unhappy. So basically, our unhappiness stems from the non-fulfilment of our aspirations and expectations, personal as well as professional.

In our constant materialistic competition and unmet personal expectations, we do not see that happiness lies in the simplest of things. Everything becomes simple when we are ready to embrace what we have in our hands and look for happiness in the imperfections in them. But by the time we do realize our folly, we lose what does matter after all.

Over the years, I have slowly understood the meaning of happiness. No, I am not an expert. I am still learning to be in charge of my emotions and reactions. I still have a long way to go. Finding happiness is a personal journey and every journey is unique. As I am growing older, and hopefully wiser, I am understanding certain aspects of happiness. Like what works and what doesn't, what helps and what doesn't. I am sharing my notes with you, in the hope that they will help you to remove some stones in your path to happiness.

Stop Complaining

You can never be happy if you don't stop complaining. Complaining about things and not doing anything to change them will not take you anywhere. It will only rob you of your peace of mind and potential joy. Complaining incessantly has never turned a frown into a smile. If you can take matters into your own hands and do something about your situation, then just do it. But if you can't, stop complaining and move on. Believe me, there are thousands of people who have it worse than you. So, you need to stop cribbing about your life and things around you right now.

Count Your Blessings

When you wake up every morning, be thankful that you are alive. Remember that thousands of people are having it worse than you. So, be thankful for whatever you have; working limbs, health, family, friends, job, a roof over your head, food on your table, people who love you and care for you, pets, or an education.

Comparing your lives with those who you assume to be better off, will only steal your happiness. Each one of us is moving on a distinct timeline. It is foolish to compare my beginning with your middle. Every one of us dreams of a perfect life which we measure according to individual happiness standards. But it is important to understand that, good things take time to happen. So be patient and remember to count your blessings every day.

Find the Humour

Life is never smooth. We will always have our ups and downs. And complaining or worrying about the downs all the time will only take us down for good. So, we should learn to smile through it and have a good laugh about it. Of course, it is not easy to find humour in our problems, but it is possible. Once you learn the art, it becomes easier. Talking from my experience here! Like we all have a handful of people in our lives who make things difficult and at times our life miserable. I say that such people are the spices of life, who give us the real taste of life.

Be Kind

Your life is not perfect. But whose is? Someone else's life may look glossy from a distance. But each one of us is fighting our own battle. So, be kind to everyone and everything around. You may not be reciprocated immediately, but like water, kindness has the power to get through the toughest of rocks. Just remember to treat others the way you want to be treated.

See The Good in People

Well, this is a tough one. How do you see good in someone who has always been bad or unkind to you? Is it even possible that people who are full of themselves have an ounce of goodness in them? It might not seem feasible, but all people have some light within them, even if it is hidden in the deepest crevices of their souls. Remember the one time (it might be several instances too) such a person has shown you some kindness and cling to it. Try to understand why he or she behaves in such a manner. If not anything else, pity them for they are losing out on so much happiness.

Forgive and Move On

This one is probably the toughest to execute. Forgiving someone who has hurt you or wronged you, either knowingly or unknowingly, is not at all easy. I often said that I had forgiven but not forgotten. But I have understood that if I haven't let it go, I have not been able to forgive at all. Holding on to grudges gives you sleepless nights, irritable days, a turbulent mind, and a bitter heart and tongue. Trust me, it's no good. In the recent past, I had spent a good amount of time thinking and talking about old and fresh resentments or bitterness and doomed myself. So, forgive and move on.

Invest in Relationships

Acquiring wealth and success are not keys to a happy and healthy life. One may have all material comfort and luxury in the world but might be the unhappiest and loneliest being on earth. If we don't have anyone to share our success and wealth with, what is the use of slogging day and night. This period of the pandemic has shown us the importance of good health and healthy relationships, be it with family or friends.

Stay Healthy

A healthy mind is directly proportional to a healthy body and vice-versa. You don't feel good if your body doesn't and your body doesn't feel good if your mind is not at peace. Taking care of your body is the first step to a healthy life, and if you take care of your body, it will in turn take care of you.

Find a Hobby

I believe it is necessary to have hobbies. In case you are wondering, making other people's lives difficult and gossiping does not count as hobbies. An idle mind is a devil's workshop. Hobbies help keep our minds occupied and away from negative thoughts. They help us unwind and de-stress and promote a sense of positivity. Our hobbies can significantly contribute towards our health, mental as well as physical. With hobbies, our happiness is not linked to the physical presence of others all the time. It is like spending time with oneself and feeling content.

Feel His Presence

When I pray, I talk to Him. When I am happy, I thank Him. When I am worried, I plea to Him. When I am sad, I ask Him for strength. When I look around, I see His miracles in all His creations. When something happens or doesn't happen, I try to see His reason in it, and I often understand it. When I count my blessings, I always mutter thanks to Him.

I believe that finding happiness is a continuous process. Once you get the basics right, it is easier to keep on track. I am not saying that material aspirations are not important. They are, but their fulfilment should not be directly proportional to your happiness quotient. Life is connected to life itself. Hence, happiness is more about connections with your inner self, with people in your life, with nature. Happiness can be achieved in living relationships, in stopping and smelling the roses, in dancing in the rain, in doing what you love, in kindness, in gratefulness, and in being in awe of the vast and mighty universe.

Glossary

Aita: Maternal grandmother (can refer to grandmother on either side)

Deta (Deuta): Father

Koka: Maternal grandfather (can refer to a grandfather on either side)

Ma: Mother